E. ROBERT BROOKS

Other Publications by E. Robert Brooks
Pirouette
Derailed Gears
The Concours Caper

Publishing Coordinator – Sharon Kizziah-Holmes

Paperback-Press
an imprint of A & S Publishing
A & S Holmes, Inc.

ISBN -13: 978-1-956806-23-6

DEDICATION

Jane Gregory Brooks- A gifted writer, who sought to teach me about the importance of correct grammar and syntax, and an appreciation for style

Peter G. Rudiger- My first vinous mentor, who educated me about the intricacies of the wine trade, and instilled in me a reverence for the wines of Burgundy

PROLOGUE

*"If we sip the wine, we find dreams coming upon us
out of the imminent night."
D.H. Lawrence*

The coroner's report stated that Maurice Blanchard, who was the winemaker at the *Chateau de La Rochepot*, had died by misadventure. His death was ruled an accidental drowning.

He had apparently become disoriented due to the heady effects from excessive inhalation of intoxicating fumes, which were the byproduct of a vigorous vinous fermentation.

It was postulated that he must have slipped and fallen into the frothy liquid, while he was in the process of punching down the cap of sediment in a large ancient open top wooden cask.

In his encumbered state, he had been unable to climb out.

His body was found the next morning floating amongst the lees.

CHAPTER ONE

"Wine makes a man more pleased with himself, I do not say that it makes him more pleasing to others."
Samuel Johnson

Near the Burgundian town of Beaune, lies the hamlet of La Rochepot.
Home to the grand 12th century *Chateau de La Rochepot*, which, like many such castles, had been built upon the ruins of another.

Originally called *Chateau de La Roche-Nolay*, it was renamed in 1403 by a crusader knight- Régnier Pot, when he became the new proprietor.

Under his ownership Pinot Noir grapes were planted, since the cultivation of Gamay grapes in Burgundy had been outlawed in 1395.

In the ensuing years, the *Chateau* changed hands several times.

During the French Revolution, it was renamed *Chateau de La Roche-Fidele*, and the property subsequently fell into disrepair.

In 1893, the estate was purchased by the family of the president of the Republic of France- Sadi Carnot.

The name of the property reverted to *Chateau de La Rochepot*, and the buildings were sympathetically and carefully restored by his son over the course of twenty-six years, to return them to their former glory.

According to some of the more vociferous inhabitants of this small village, the new owner of the *Chateau de La Rochepot*—Hans Gauner, who had relocated from Germany—was a mysterious man.

A chemist by training and trade, he was a reclusive millionaire who had made his fortune by mixing and supplying exotic fragrances to several of the most renowned international luxury perfume brands.

The residents assumed that he had purchased the property as a trophy of his prosperity.

M. Gauner was clearly an interloper, and worse yet, a foreigner from a country for which many Frenchmen still held deep-seated resentments from the legacy of the war.

Upon his arrival in La Rochepot, he was studiously shunned with silent prejudice by the judgmental indigenous denizens, and not welcomed into their society.

Nor did he appear to make any effort to ingratiate himself with them, or with the local winemaking fraternity.

His comings and goings were shrouded in secrecy.

He would arrive at the castle at odd hours,

whisking by the surrounding properties in his vintage Rolls-Royce, with nary a greeting or acknowledgement of his neighbors as he passed them by.

Often, he was glimpsed with his protégé, a man known as *Le Nez*, who was revered as an expert in the perfume trade, and reputed to possess an incredible olfactory skill.

This notoriety earned *Le Nez* a grudging respect from local winemakers, albeit from afar, since it was alleged that he was capable of accurately identifying hundreds of different scents.

Unlike the spacious and elaborate above-ground *chais* at many top Bordeaux *chateaux*, which are homages to the wealth of the proprietors, even at the best properties in Burgundy, wine is customarily stored in more utilitarian underground cellars.

For Gauner and his staff, the subterranean space at the *Chateau de La Rochepot*, was an ideal location to conduct their oenological experiments in complete privacy.

CHAPTER TWO

"A bottle of wine contains more philosophy than all the books in the world."
Louis Pasteur

For centuries, Bordeaux and Burgundy have vied to be recognized as the preeminent wine region of France, but Bordeaux has always enjoyed several advantages not afforded to Burgundy.

From 1152 to 1453, Bordeaux was under British rule.

The British gentry developed a taste for the local wines, which they referred to as *Claret*.

Given Bordeaux's proximity to the Atlantic Ocean and the British Isles, the region had a long tradition of overseas trade.

Expatriate Brits, as well as Protestant Irish, Scots, Danes, Dutch and Germans, came to Bordeaux in the

18th century, and they opened successful *négociant* wine trading companies along the *Quai-de-Chartrons*.

These merchants, who became known as *Chartrons*, were practical and pragmatic businessmen steeped in the culture of commerce.

Though not accepted into the society of the indigenous elite Catholic landowners and grape growers, who nonetheless became dependent on them to purchase their wines, they prospered.

Eventually, many of these affluent merchant princes used their newfound wealth to also become chateau owners.

While not as grandiose as the castle-like *chateaux* in the Loire Valley, the *chateaux*, or mansions of Bordeaux, are impressive.

With generally much larger vineyards than those in Burgundy, over time these properties tended to stay much more intact, as a legacy of primogeniture through the British influence, which provided that the eldest son inherited all the family real estate.

Whereas in Catholic Burgundy, the accepted practice, ever since Napoleonic inheritance laws, was that all the children received a portion of the family property.

As a result, vineyards in Burgundy were divided into many small parcels through the years.

In some of the vineyards, owners have only a row or two of grapevines, and the yields are miniscule compared to typical production in Bordeaux.

Historically, there were very few *domaines* in Burgundy that made and bottled their own wines.

Most grape growers, especially those with small

holdings, sold their grapes to *négociants*, who would then make the wines and bottle them.

The estates in Bordeaux, as a rule, began the practice of bottling their own wines decades earlier than Burgundy, once local laws were passed mandating that.

Burgundy is also fundamentally different from Bordeaux in other ways.

The region is geographically landlocked and lacks a major trade route.

The inhabitants are by nature and inclination more insular.

Most Burgundians, raised for generations in their well-entrenched local culture, and influenced by a significant church presence and vineyard ownership, would never think to purchase or imbibe any wine produced outside of their borders, much less willingly tolerate an outsider.

Even citizens from nearby Alsace were often avoided, and privately considered to be more German than French, despite their protests to the contrary.

CHAPTER THREE

"In victory you deserve Champagne. In defeat, you need it."
Napoleon Bonaparte

While under occupation during World War II, the *Bordelaise* suffered the indignity of having to tolerate the top *chateaux* being commandeered by the German High Command as headquarters for their various military branches.

As part of their overall meticulous advance planning, the senior Nazi officers had determined which chateaux they would occupy, not based on militaristic strategy, location, or facilities infrastructure, but motivated by which wines they most appreciated and coveted.

Under their less than benign auspices, vintages

bottled at those *chateaux* during that time carried the addition of swastika symbols on the capsules.

While so entrenched, the Germans entertained lavishly and consumed prized vintages as often as possible.

But at one of these prominent estates, they failed to find many of the most ancient rarities that had been secretly stored in a small cellar behind a large false cask with a hidden door.

The winery staff had also placed stacks of wooden cases in front of the cask just before the invaders arrived.

One frequent guest to their elaborate dinners was a Vichy collaborator named Maurice Papon, who at that time was second-in-charge of the Gironde region.

After the war, he continued to advance his political career for many years, and he held several prestigious posts in French government including roles as Paris police chief, member of parliament, and budget minister.

But eventually justice was served, and he was belatedly tried and convicted of war crimes as the highest ranking Frenchman guilty of complicity in crimes against humanity.

Burgundy also had its share of Nazi collaborators.

Winemaker Bernard Grivelet spent time in prison after the war for his role in supplying wine to the occupiers.

Like others who were similarly accused, he contended that he was innocent.

Not long after his release, Grivelet was involved in a wine scandal in the late 1950s...

CHAPTER FOUR

"Compromises are for relationships, not wine."
Sir Robert Caywood

In the aftermath of the Second World War, Europe's manufacturing capabilities had been largely decimated. Substantial infusions of American money to rebuild factories and infrastructure in France, courtesy of the Marshall Plan, resulted in all new state-of-the-art equipment and technology for industries such as ship and airplane construction.

Wine production facilities, on the other hand, had to largely make do with existing, and often antiquated equipment.

Even in the 1970s, many French wineries still used old cement vats and bottling machines that had been in use since the early 1930s.

But the postwar years were filled with extraordinary French vintages.

Throughout the latter part of the 1940s, as well as in the 1950s and 1960s, many legendary wines were produced.

Sales and revenues increased dramatically, and influenced by growing demand and newfound affluence, many wineries expanded and increased production.

The 1970s also saw some fine vintages, which prompted further price escalation and unprecedented market speculation.

However, years later, a number of very competent winemakers were unfairly criticized about their wines from the 1970s by some journalists and consumers who perceived a decline in winemaking quality for those vintages, as well as significant bottle variation and a lack of longevity.

That inconsistency, and those disappointments, were in fact often due instead to poor provenance because of a lack of proper temperature control during shipping and subsequent storage conditions.

This perception was also influenced by comparisons to wines produced in the 1980s, when the effects of global warming were already beginning to be a consideration with earlier harvests and higher alcohol levels.

Winemaking techniques had begun to come into vogue that prioritized a more sensational and international style, rather than reflecting the influences and subtleties of local terroirs.

As these wines from the 1970s aged, critics who did not have extensive experience with mature wines failed to recognize that over the course of a wine's evolution, it is not unusual for it to close down at certain stages, only to afterwards reemerge with greater complexity and nuanced flavor than the previous level of development.

It is certainly factual that in the 1970s some wineries experienced fluctuations in quality due to poor winemaking and vineyard practices, and expanded production.

Stylistically, many French wines in those days often tended to be more restrained with an emphasis on elegance and finesse, rather than sheer power, overt ripeness and intensity.

They were also more variable from vintage-to-vintage because they more accurately reflected the variations of the weather, rather than the influences of oenological manipulations in the *cuveries*.

It is also true that slick marketing executives, transplanted from the food branding industry, promoted the notion of uniformity and absolute clarity of the wine in the bottle being desirable attributes to attract American consumers.

In response, some wineries adopted the detrimental practice of pasteurizing their wines, as well as excessive filtering and centrifuging.

The 1970s also brought two massive French wine scandals involving the mislabeling of highly regarded French wine.

The first was a well-publicized fraud in 1973, dubbed *Winegate*, involving Lionel Cruse of the formerly highly respected négociant firm of *Cruse et Fils Fréres*, that had been founded by his forebears in 1819.

This troubling revelation threatened to implode the highly inflated market for Bordeaux wines.

Throughout France, the practice of illegally blending fine wines with cheaper varieties was certainly not unprecedented, and had, *behind-the-scenes*, been an accepted practice by some members of the wine trade for many years.

In the early 1970s, there were hundreds of proven violations of the French wine laws, but so long as the fines were quietly collected, the authorities were placated, and generally no one paid much attention.

The Cruse controversy, however, involved two million bottles of wine falsely labeled as Bordeaux that had been blended with wines from the Midi region.

The scale of this fraud and resultant negative publicity disrupted the French wine trade at a level never seen before.

What Cruse had done was clearly in violation of the strict French wine authenticity laws, but he and his team of legal experts claimed as their main defense, that the inferior and less expensive Midi wines sold as more prestigious Bordeaux were actually superior in quality to what the labels indicated.

They claimed innocence because they had ostensibly provided their customers with a better product!

Allegedly, none of these wines ever reached the American market because the French government claimed that all the bottles had been impounded by their revenue agents before shipment.

However, the seeds of distrust were planted. For a time anyway, many American consumers lost faith in Bordeaux wine, and in hindsight they wondered how many cases of illegally blended and mislabeled wine had previously been sold to them undetected...

CHAPTER FIVE

"God made only water, but man-made wine."
Victor Hugo

A s a young man entering the wine trade, I made the requisite pilgrimage to France to visit the fabled wine regions.

My first experience was working the harvest at a preeminent Bordeaux chateau.

When I arrived at their vineyards, I was surprised to see technicians who were clinically attired in blue lab coats and rubber boots.

They busily consulted aerial thermal imagery of the vineyards and examined spectrometer readings to scientifically determine optimal harvest conditions.

Meanwhile, I noticed a spry elderly gentleman walking through the vineyard rows.

Studiously ignoring the comments and conclusions of the technicians, he gazed intently at the sky to evaluate the weather, and stopped from time to time to pick a grape and taste it.

After a few minutes, I overheard him declare to himself that picking would commence in three days.

His sage proclamation reminded me of the time-honored proverb- being in the right place at the right time is luck, but knowing that you are there is skill!

I subsequently learned that this man was the patriarch of the estate.

He had lived through the war and was of the old school.

He had relinquished many of the day-to-day business activities to his son, who was fixated on embracing modern precepts and technology.

But every day during the harvest, Le Patron, as he was called by the employees at the winery, would habitually appear at mid-morning astride his ancient upright bicycle, en route home from the *boulangerie* in the local village, always with a *baguette* of newly baked bread perched on the pannier rack behind his saddle.

Garbed in his customary attire of a tweed jacket with a colorful ascot and jaunty beret, he would dismount for a walking tour of the vineyards.

The vineyards were impeccably maintained with all the vines carefully pruned and manicured.

Roses planted at the ends of the rows appeared to be purely decorative, but they in fact served a very practical purpose as an early warning system for the health of the vines, since the flowers were more sensitive and reacted much more quickly to diseases.

The gravelly ground epitomized the old wise adage that the poorer the soil, the better the wine, because the vine roots delve more deeply for nourishment in order to survive.

The experience of tasting great old vintages produced from these vineyards confirmed to me- out of adversity, comes greatness.

Much like his cherished ancient grapevines, the proprietor's roots to this land ran deep through several generations.

At the time that I worked there, his brokerage company was one of the largest in the Bordeaux wine trade, and his family also owned several *chateaux*, of which this property was the most prestigious.

After the harvest was completed, I spent several months working at their offices and winery in the city of Bordeaux.

Among the tasks I was involved in was the selection of wines to be served aboard the ultra-modern French-built Concorde jet airplanes.

In contrast, the winery equipment dated back to the days of biplane aircraft.

At that time, the Place Gambetta plaza was traditionally where residents and tourists gathered for shopping and dining, and I spent much of my leisure time there with my colleagues.

These days, the *Quai-de-Chartrons* district, where the *négociant* warehouses are located, has been re-envisioned and transformed into an upscale retail destination with boutique stores and restaurants.

Unfortunately for the family, the formerly

profitable *négociant* business had seriously suffered from the precipitous market decline caused by the Lionel Cruse scandal.

Facing ever-mounting expenses with greatly reduced revenues, they nonetheless honorably paid all their financial commitments.

But to do so, they were forced in the year after I departed to sell their best chateau to a wealthy Parisian grocery company.

Of course this was not the first time that wealthy individuals and large cash rich companies had invested in Bordeaux estates, but this trend of turnover accelerated over the next decade, resulting in many of the established wine families quietly fading into obscurity, or accepting subordinate roles.

However, significant improvements were made to many vineyards and cellars that had previously languished due to a lack of adequate operating capital.

CHAPTER SIX

"When it came to writing about wine, I did what
almost everybody does—faked it."
Art Buchwald

In 1979, just when the public was beginning to
forget about *Winegate*, along came a new scandal,
this time involving France's other great wine
region—Burgundy.

The quantity of wine involved was far less than in
the Cruse Bordeaux scandal, but this case had an even
more serious impact on the imported wine trade in
America.

Interest and sales of fine wine had grown
exponentially in the United States in the ensuing
years, and unlike the Cruse scheme where the
fraudulent wines were purportedly impounded and
never reached American consumers, 70,000 bottles of

intentionally mislabeled wines were shipped to the United States, and distributed at what appeared to be bargain prices. Not surprisingly, they sold out quickly.

Historically, lovers of Burgundy wine have often overlooked winemaking improprieties that blatantly flaunted the rules, so long as the results were palatable.

Many connoisseurs savored the Averys Burgundies, which had benefited from the addition of fruit liqueur, and the Docteur Barolet wines, which had been augmented with brandy.

But those infractions were intended to improve and preserve the wines.

This current abuse of the law was a much different case.

Bernard Grivelet, of Nazi collaborator infamy, who had previously been charged with fraud in Burgundy in the 1950s, and then disappeared from the wine scene for several years- had subsequently returned.

He was now the owner of a small, but well-known Burgundian estate and brokerage company, which was well represented in the United States by prominent fine wine importer- Frederick Wildman and Sons.

Grivelet was indicted for labeling and selling wines of dubious origin as famed Premier and Grand Cru Burgundies.

The Grivelet affair aroused great concern in the Burgundy wine trade, whose practices had long been viewed with suspicion by many knowledgeable buyers around the world.

Of the French wine regions, Burgundy had by far

the worst reputation for fraud.

The *Comité Interprofessionel-des-Vins-de-Bourgogne* (CIVB) alleged that instances of fraud in Burgundy were extremely rare, but M. Grivelet's defense was that, "What I did is done every day.

"The papers are straightened out; sometimes a small fine is paid, and that is the end of it."

Contrary to the claims of the CIVB, subsequent revelations about malfeasance by other high-profile members of the Burgundy wine trade soon shed further light on the rampant extent of fraud in this region.

At the beginning of the 1980s, the trend of substantial investment by ultra-rich individuals and large corporations in French vineyard properties continued, with both under-performing and famed estates changing ownership.

In most instances, this was beneficial to the overall quality of the wines, but sometimes it resulted in a more corporate than artisanal approach to the winemaking.

Prices for *blue chip* wines continued to escalate, and in America, among high-level collectors, concerns about fraudulent rarities became more pronounced and prevalent.

Previously, wine fraud had primarily been concentrated on relatively inexpensive commodity wines sold in volume.

Just a few months into the new decade, another major scandal in Burgundy was uncovered.

This time it involved nearly half a million cases of fraudulent white wine.

Americans had developed a fixation for Pouilly-Fuissé, and many clever merchants had taken advantage of this trend, often selling mediocre examples for inflated prices.

But one unscrupulous exporter hatched a scheme to profit even more.

He sent ordinary French white table wine to Holland for bottling.

From there, it was shipped to England to be fictitiously labeled as Pouilly-Fuissé under the Michelet and Alfred Montigny brands.

During this time, much greater quantities of so-called Pouilly-Fuissé were sold in America than the region produced.

Many in the wine business who knew about this, even if they were not directly involved, still shared culpability because they chose to ignore it.

Though the Grivelet, Michelet and Montigny scandals initially received a lot of publicity and prompted consumer outrage, official investigations of illegal practices in the wine trade were generally avoided.

The wine-buying public usually remained blissfully ignorant of these vinous manipulations.

Even ethical and honest *vignerons* and *négociants* did not want to be involved in discussions about wine fraud because the subject was bad for business.

But wine scandals in Burgundy were far from over...

CHAPTER SEVEN

"Wine is bottled poetry."
Robert Louis Stevenson

The second destination of my vinous education about famed French wines took me to Burgundy.

Here I encountered an enthusiastic group of young scions of famous winemaking families who were beginning to make their mark in the region.

They aspired to make high quality wines with an artisanal approach, which juxtaposed against some of the entrenched *négociant* companies that were focused instead on volume production, and making their businesses as lucrative as possible.

This new generation of vineyard owners and winemakers embraced a return to organic and biodynamic cultivation methods.

But their inspiration was only in part due to an acknowledgment of nature's holistic influences on viniculture, such as the effects from changing ocean tides and phases of the moon.

Their motivation had primarily been dictated by the pragmatic realization that the harsh chemical weed-killers, fertilizers, and pesticides that had been used for the past decade were literally destroying the soil.

On a more personal level their choice became even more fundamental.

A deeply disturbing realization that some of the people working in these vineyards, as well as the children playing near them, had been contaminated, and were dying from cancers and other diseases caused by these products.

It would be easy to blame the previous generation of *vignerons* for embracing the use of these virulent substances, but despite the perception that winemaking is a glamorous career, any agricultural business entails substantial risk and uncertainty.

After too often suffering the vicissitudes of blights and capricious weather, often with the associated looming possibility for financial ruin, these conscientious wine growers were not to be blamed for the temptation to embrace the promise of higher yields and more reliable harvests by using these so-called wonder treatments.

But now their children saw the wisdom of returning to the non-interventionist techniques and vineyard stewardship of their wise grandfathers and great-grandfathers.

However, even some treatments allowed under organic practices are controversial.

Copper sulfate, which has been used on grapevines for decades, and is allowed for use in organic farming, is a protective fungicide for treating downy mildew.

When used, a bluish residue is visible on the leaves.

The traditional Bordeaux mixture is a combination with lime and water.

For workers applying it, it can be a severe eye irritant, and can cause liver and kidney damage.

In extreme cases, shock and death can occur. Children are especially sensitive.

It is also very toxic to fish, birds and honeybees, and accumulated copper deposits can create lifeless soil and toxic residue in groundwater.

Several volume wine producers have been known to use copper sulfate for another purpose as well.

Prior to harvest, they spray it on the vines to create the perception in the resultant wine of greater complexity of flavor due to more prevalent tannins.

Some people are sensitive and allergic to sulfites.

Sulfites are typically added as a preservative to many foods, and are a natural byproduct of fermentation.

All wines contain sulfites. Sulfites have been added to wine as a preservative for thousands of years to prevent browning and discoloration from spoilage and oxidation, and to keep bacteria and yeasts from growing.

In Europe, even organic wines usually have small levels of added sulfites.

Especially white wines which do not have the

tannin that is present in red wines. Tannin acts as a natural antioxidant.

Sulfites are also used for sweet wines to prevent secondary fermentation of the remaining sugar.

Conversely, red wines have more allergy-causing histamines, and headache-causing tyramines, than white wines.

Sparkling wines generally don't need added sulfites, because the carbon dioxide which provides the effervescence also acts as a natural antioxidant.

Vignerons in Burgundy typically age many wines in barrels, but not adding any sulfites to barrel-aged wine increases the likelihood of detrimental oxidization, because over time minute amounts of oxygen seep into barrels through the pores in the wood.

It was during this initial tour of Burgundy that I first met Pierre Ducler, while dining one evening with new wine friends.

Pierre was the *sommelier* at a prestigious Michelin three-star restaurant in Lyon.

I immediately enjoyed and appreciated his affable nature and considerable wine knowledge, and over the ensuing years, we became close friends.

The restaurant was world-renowned for both its *haute cuisine*, and the extensive Burgundy wine collection.

During our initial conversation, Pierre shared that the highlight of his occupation was the opportunity to regularly sample rarities that wealthy customers ordered, which he could never personally afford.

One such customer was *in situ* that evening,

conspicuously holding court with his entourage.

His name, I learned from Pierre, was Hans Gauner, and he was reputed to be a wine collector of some renown.

At one point in the evening, Herr Gauner was speaking with Pierre, and upon learning that there were several young winemakers and a wine broker at our table, he invited us to join him.

Though we had already begun our dinner, Pierre and our waiter graciously accommodated us, and we joined Gauner for our remaining courses.

Herr Gauner was very generous to share some exceptional older Burgundies, including an extraordinary 1964 Chambertin, and throughout the evening he asked us for our opinions, and inquired about my friends wine-making philosophies and techniques. He was a polite and studious listener.

We talked about the fact that wines always taste better in the location where they are made, because in that environment you are breathing in the scents of the indigenous air and soil.

We discussed wine affinities—that the tannins in red wines match well with proteins in meats and cheeses, and cause the wines to taste rounder and more supple; that the salinity in shellfish is synergistic with the bracing acidity in white wines like Chablis.

The broker quoted a time-honored saying from the wine trade, "buy with apples; sell with cheese."

I had become engrossed in their conversation, and it wasn't until we had finished our fish course that I noticed that while my plate revealed an untidy pile of bones pushed ignominiously to the side, on all of the other diner's dishes, the exposed skeletal structures conspicuously remained perfectly intact.

When Herr Gauner glanced at my plate, his hooded reproving look conveyed the opinion that his American guest lacked cultural decorum and refinement...

CHAPTER EIGHT

"Life is too short to drink bad wine."
Unknown

In 1985, two new major scandals sent shockwaves throughout the wine world, this time emanating from Austria, Germany and Italy.

One involved celebrated forged historic rarities, that would live on in ignominy in fine wine aficionado's memories for decades.

The other, which was far more extensive, and required the destruction of thirty-six million bottles of tainted wine that were potentially harmful to the health of consumers worldwide, was inexplicably quickly forgotten in only a few short years by the majority of wine purchasers.

Meinhard Görke was a flashy showman and promoter, who changed his name to Hardy

Rodenstock in the 1970s when he started working in the music business managing popular rock bands. At that time, he developed a keen interest in fine wines. In the early 1980s, he began orchestrating and hosting remarkable tastings in Germany which featured spectacular old rarities.

These high-profile events, which were attended by renowned wine trade professionals, noted collectors and celebrities, brought him international recognition.

Frequent guests included influential wine writers and critics—Michael Broadbent MW, Jancis Robinson MW, and Robert Parker of Wine Advocate fame.

Prominent winery owners such as Denis Durantou, Comte Alexandre-De-Lur-Saluces and Angelo Gaja also attended, as well as high-end wineglass maker Georg Riedel.

Rodenstock gained further global attention in 1985 when he announced that he had discovered a secret walled-off cellar in a Paris basement, that contained bottles of Châteaux Lafite, Margaux, d'Yquem and Branne-Mouton (Mouton-Rothschild), from the 1784 and 1787 vintages, all marked with the engraved initials Th J.

Rodenstock alleged that these wines had been bottled for the well-known oenophile and US president—Thomas Jefferson.

Maurice Renaud, a well-regarded French wine broker, who at that time was generally acknowledged as the preeminent private vendor in Paris for rare wines, was mystified that such a collection could exist without his knowledge...

Later that year at a Christie's wine auction in London, a bottle of Th J 1787 Chateau Lafite was sold for the world-record price of $157,000 to the Forbes publishing family.

Wine Spectator publisher- Marvin Shanken, bought a half bottle of Th J 1784 Chateau Margaux for $30,000 at another Christie's auction in 1987.

Michael Broadbent had tasted a small sample from the bottle and assessed the wine to still be sound.

In 1989, flamboyant New York wine merchant- William Sokolin, acquired on consignment from a London dealer a bottle of Th J 1787 Chateau Margaux.

He brought the bottle to a posh event celebrating Chateau Margaux at the Four Seasons hotel, and while showing it to the attendees, he accidentally dropped and broke it.

Energy magnate and avid wine collector- Bill Koch, purchased four of the Jefferson bottles in the late 1980s for a total of a half-million dollars.

For several years, Rodenstock's by now-fabled tastings continued- including a vertical of Chateau Petrus, with all the vintages poured from Imperial size bottles, and an unprecedented 125 vintage vertical of Château d'Yquem.

Tracing the provenance of older wines is not an exact science.

Accurate bottling and sales records at some properties are often scarce, or non-existent.

In many instances, before estate bottling became common practice, a number of wineries would sell barrels of wine to merchants who did the bottling.

Occasionally, on request, a winery would combine the contents of several regular bottles to fill a large format bottle for a client or friend's special event.

But the improbability of the existence of some of the old rarities at the Rodenstock tastings having been bottled in large format bottles caused suspicion by a few wine experts who attended these grandiose events.

During this time, American collectors made headlines purchasing many other fabled rarities, including large format bottles, for stratospheric prices from auctions and high-end retailers.

Most notably from Royal Wine Merchants in New York City.

Many of these wines were subsequently traced back to Rodenstock.

In 2005, Bill Koch tried to exhibit his four Jefferson bottles of Lafite and Branne-Mouton at the Boston Museum of Fine Arts.

In preparation for the exhibition, the museum contacted the Thomas Jefferson Foundation at Monticello to verify the provenance of the wines.

But based on the Foundation's extensive review of their archived documents, they concluded that these bottles were likely fakes.

An outraged and understandably vindictive Koch, began a long and well-publicized legal battle with Rodenstock, that continued for several years.

Even though Koch hired a small army of noted experts to gather evidence and support his case, he was thwarted by Rodenstock's refusal to answer legal summons and appear in a United States court of law.

Among these experts was Philippe Hubert, a French physicist who subjected the contents of these bottles to low-level gamma ray detection for cesium 137 to attempt to date the age of the wines, and scientifically determine if they predated the nuclear bomb detonations of 1945.

In a significant setback for Koch, after the tests were concluded Hubert stated that, "Unfortunately, we could not detect any cesium inside the wine."

So, it was certain that the wines had been bottled before the Atomic Age.

But there was no way that these tests could accurately prove the exact age of the wines, and whether or not they had been bottled during Jefferson's lifetime.

Prior to the 1985 London auction of the first Jefferson bottle, experts at Christies had examined and tested some of the Th J bottles, and opined that the engravings appeared to be authentic, but Koch's investigators succeeded to track down associates of Rodenstock's in Germany who contradicted that opinion.

Koch's investigators testified that Rodenstock's accomplices had engraved the so-called Jefferson bottles with the Th J lettering using a modern motorized dental tool, that could not possibly have existed in the time of Thomas Jefferson.

Despite this evidence, Rodenstock was never formally criminally arraigned, or found guilty of fraud in the United States.

A civil judge awarded a default judgment in Koch's favor, but Rodenstock never paid any restitution or fines.

However, in 1992 Rodenstock was accused in Germany of selling fake wines by a former friend and customer named Hans-Peter Fredricks.

The case was brought to trial and the presiding judge found Rodenstock guilty.

But Rodenstock appealed the decision, and the participants agreed to settle out of court.

Just as with Pouilly-Fuissé from France, the wines from the town of Piesport in the Mosel region of Germany were hugely popular in 1980s America, and it was common knowledge in the wine trade that unscrupulous dealers were selling larger quantities of Piesporter Goldtropfchen and Piesporter Michelsberg than those areas produced.

Wines from nearby lesser-known vineyards that tasted similar, but did not command the same high prices, were conveniently transformed via falsified documents and labels to satisfy the thirst for Piesporter, and provide substantial illicit profits.

But this chicanery paled in comparison to the new frauds that were revealed in Austria and Germany.

A chemist in Austria named Otto Nadrasky, who was a consultant for several large wineries, had concocted a method to increase profits for his clients.

Wine laboratories performing quality controls on Austrian and German wines sold in West Germany discovered that some wines were adulterated with a toxic substance—diethylene glycol, one of the main ingredients in automotive antifreeze.

This ingredient was being used in Austria to make wines appear sweeter and fuller-bodied, to resemble more expensive late-harvest wines.

Many of these adulterated Austrian wines were exported to Germany in bulk where they were illegally blended into German wines by importers.

Dozens of wine producers and brokers were arrested in Austria, and fines were levied in Germany as well, with key managers of the large wholesale dealer and bottler Pieroth also sentenced.

But the repercussions were not limited to trials, fines and prison sentences for the guilty offenders.

The magnitude of affected wines caused a complete collapse of the Austrian wine export business.

Austrian wines were banned in many countries around the world, and the reputation for German wines suffered significantly as well.

While the German wine business recovered in only a few years, the commerce in Austrian wines took over a decade to rebuild.

In the meantime, the winemaking focus in Austria changed for the better, from late-harvest style wines, to predominantly dryer wines.

At the time that it occurred, the diethylene glycol exposé was the biggest scandal ever experienced in the wine business, with millions of possibly toxic bottles involved and destroyed.

But inexplicably, most consumers soon forgot this egregious debacle.

Italy, which is the world's biggest producer and exporter of wine, with over a billion dollars in annual revenues, was also implicated in this scandal.

An independent investigation was launched by a group of Massachusetts-based scientists after trace amounts of diethylene glycol were found in contaminated bottles of Riunite wine imported into the United States.

Riunite was one of the biggest selling wine brands in America.

The brand owner- *Cantine Cooperative Riunite*, of Reggio Emilia, voluntarily recalled more than 1.2 million cases.

The findings from the research team indicated that coolant from a refrigerated tank had seeped into recently pressed grape juice through a tiny hole.

The leak was repaired, and the diethylene glycol coolant was replaced with an ethylene glycol formulation that was similar in content to that commonly used by many US wineries.

The importer of Riunite- Villa Banfi, released statements from two of the researchers, that stated that wine with a level of diethylene glycol of 10 parts per million was not harmful. "A consumer who drank wine containing this small amount of diethylene glycol would not have experienced any adverse health effects," stated Professor Mark Cullen.

However, the Bureau of Alcohol, Tobacco and Firearms went on record to say that even small quantities of diethylene glycol can cause liver and kidney damage, and that larger quantities can be fatal.

Other Italian wineries, including *F Ili Dogliani*, FDO, and Spabis, were also implicated in the scandal, with wines from several prominent and prestigious regions testing positive for diethylene glycol content.

Immediately on the heels of the diethylene glycol scandal, another even more troubling exposé rocked

Italy in 1986.

In an effort to expediently raise alcohol content for inexpensive commodity wines, over sixty wineries had been found to be adulterating wine with methyl alcohol, also known as methanol, which is commonly used as a paint thinner, and is poisonous.

This contamination resulted in over twenty fatalities, as well as instances of comas and blindness.

Italy was forced to temporarily suspend and freeze all wine exports, narrowly avoiding a fate as devastating as that just recently experienced by the Austrian wine producers.

A number of European countries banned Italian wine imports and destroyed millions of gallons of Italian wine.

Noted Italian wine expert, author, and merchant-Burton Anderson wrote, "There is little doubt this is the worst wine crisis ever.

"There have been wine crises before, adulterations of the product, but never with this many dead."

Just as with the diethylene glycol scandal, worldwide wine consumers proved to have short memories.

The methyl alcohol furor was soon forgotten, and brisk Italian wine sales resumed.

Years later I learned that while still living in Germany, Hans Gauner had closely followed the news about these scandals, and he vividly remembered the details.

CHAPTER NINE

"Making good wine is a skill. Fine wine is an art."
Robert Mondavi

The 1990s heralded increased interest in organic and biodynamic methods of viniculture.
This period also saw the emergence of California *cult wines* that were stylistically similar to wines made by the self-proclaimed *garagistes* in Bordeaux, who also came to prominence at that time.

These mavericks epitomized a philosophical change to an international winemaking style that for many traditionalists eschewed refinement, elegance, and subtleties of terroir, instead favoring a homogenized style that emphasized excessive extraction, and ripe bold primary fruit flavors- hedonism in a bottle.

This "modern" winemaking approach, was also

championed by some globe-trotting *hired gun* contract consultants, who would scientifically formulate and blend a wine to be commercially successful, and to appeal to influential journalists, so that it would receive high scores and awards.

For all their feigned sophistication, many of the new young wine aficionados were single-mindedly focused on highly extracted wines with early drinkability.

They didn't understand, nor care to understand, age-worthy wines that were tannic and backward, and lacked charm in their youth because they were crafted to evolve over time.

They had no patience or interest to wait for wines to fully mature, even though experience over time invariably enhances the level of appreciation.

More enlightened connoisseurs were sometimes mistakenly judged to be elitist, because they were students of history, and had learned and preached patience to wait and drink wines when they were at an optimum age and phase of maturity.

For these oenophiles, great winemakers were artists who aspired to create wines that were legacies for future generations to enjoy.

Of course, opening older bottles is more of a gamble.

When they prove to be past their prime, or unsound, they are especially disappointing due to the significant expectations, and because of the ever-escalating acquisition prices.

There is more variability with age. The time-honored wisdom is that there are no great wines, only great bottles.

But even wines which have passed their prime can provide insights and education, and still offer a glimpse of former greatness, if the taster is willing to be truly objective and overlook flaws.

The controversy over making wines in a modern fruit-driven style, intended for early drinkability, versus more traditional wines, that perhaps better reflect their sense of place, and are crafted with a view towards enjoyment in the fullness of time, continues through the present day, with no clear resolution.

In matters of personal taste, individual palates and perceptions differ, and opinions are often subjective.

But this new-age approach has also resulted in many young wines with promising futures being imbibed prematurely.

CHAPTER TEN

"Wine makes all things possible."
George R.R. Martin

The arrival of the millennium prompted enthusiastic vinous celebrations all around the world.

But in Burgundy, it also marked the beginning of further dire announcements about major conspiracies in the local wine trade.

This time, over a million bottles of purported Premier and Grand Cru wines from the most prestigious appellations were under suspicion of having been augmented with wines from the Midi.

Local authorities under the aegis of the *Service Regional-de-La Police Judiciare* sought to generate maximum attention by announcing the charges just prior to the start of the highly publicized and well-attended annual *Hospices-de-Beaune* charity auction and tasting event, with hundreds of journalists and wine trade professionals in attendance.

Assisting the agents was an investigator who wore a dilapidated serge suit, named Claude Leveque.

Leveque was a former French customs officer, who had then worked for the European Commission at UCLAF (*Unité-de-Coordination-de-Lutte Anti-Fraude*).

When that organization was replaced by OLAF (the European Anti-Fraud Office) in 1999, Leveque joined their ranks.

OLAF is an independent Directorate of the European Commission.

One of the organization's primary tasks is to fight fraud affecting European Union budgets.

It is an administrative agency that formulates anti-fraud strategies for Member States, and helps them in their anti-fraud activities.

However, OLAF has no judicial powers to require national law enforcement agencies in the member states to act on their recommendations.

Leveque had been previously in charge of investigating cigarette smuggling throughout Europe, and the associated significant loss of Customs duty revenues.

But the ever-increasing revelations about wine fraud in Europe had finally prompted attention from OLAF, and Leveque was the agent they appointed to determine the gravity of the problem.

The crimes were committed by executives from several prominent wholesalers and merchants, including the *négociants*: *SA Goichot*, Denis Philibert—CEO of *Maison Philibert*; *Manoir-de-La Bressandihre*, *Liglise et Fils*, the brothers Francois and Philippe Morion—former owners of *Chanson Pere et Fils*, and Pierre Bitouzet—owner of *Maison et Domaine Bitouzet*, who was also a director of the well-known *Domaine Prince-de-Mérode*.

The largest bottling company in the region—*Societé-de-Bourguignonne-d'Embouteillage*—was also implicated.

The firm of Chanson, founded in 1750, had recently been sold.

Authorities learned of the alleged fraud from Chanson's new owner- *Societé Jacques Bollinger*, which also owned Champagne Bollinger, and had purchased Chanson in the Fall of 1999.

The lawyer for the Marions acknowledged that they had unquestionably committed violations against France's *appellation controleé* laws, but he alleged that in doing so, they were no different than many other *négociant*s in Burgundy.

He stated, "It's a practice that has existed for generations, and it's even more frequent now that there is a very strong international competition."

In 2005, scandal returned to Italy. Authorities in Tuscany seized the equivalent of nine million bottles of Chianti Classico, a quarter of the region's annual production, as part of a far-reaching fraud probe.

Piero Conticelli was suspected of defrauding Chianti Classico producers by selling them wine from outside the specified region.

The seized wines were tested to try and determine

whether or not they had originated from within the legally defined boundaries of black rooster designated Chianti Classico.

South Africa also became the subject of a wine scandal with news that KWV, one of the largest and best known producers in that country, had been accused of adding artificial flavoring ingredients to Sauvignon Blanc juice to enhance aromatic varietal characteristics.

In 2006, the investigations into fraud in Burgundy continued.

The well-known Beaujolais firm- *Vins Georges Duboeuf*, was found guilty and fined for illegally mixing Gamay grapes from Beaujolais-Villages with higher-priced Cru Beaujolais grapes from Brouilly, Côte-de-Brouilly, and Moulin-à-Vent.

Duboeuf was still able to sell these bottles by declassifying and labeling them instead as Beaujolais-Villages.

However, just as with Pouilly-Fuissé and Piesporter, it was generally accepted at that time, that far more Beaujolais was sold than was legally produced in the region, based on actual harvest statistics and yield limits.

In 2008, Italy once again suffered a significant wine scandal.

Twenty well-known producers of Brunello-di-Montalcino, including Argiano and *Castello Banfi*, came under suspicion of wine fraud.

The investigation was called *Brunellogate*, and it alleged that some Brunello producers had secretly and illegally added other types of grapes from southern

Italy into their wines, when by law only Sangioveto Grosso is allowed to be used.

Hundreds of thousands of bottles were seized by the investigating magistrates.

Argiano was subsequently acquitted of adulteration.

In 2012, accusations of another wine scam struck in Burgundy.

This time, *Maison Labouré-Roi*, whose top executives were the brothers Louis and Armand Cottin, and which was owned by their company *Cottin Frères*, was accused of mis-labeling 500,000 bottles of wine.

Four executives from the company, one of the largest wine producers in the region, were arrested and convicted.

Behind the scenes, Claude Leveque had coordinated the investigation.

This trial followed closely on another *cause celebré* case that received worldwide attention.

In America, a grand jury convicted high profile wine collector Rudy Kurniawan of multiple counts of fraud, in a multimillion-dollar scheme where he counterfeited thousands of bottles of expensive rare old wines in the makeshift laboratory he had created in the kitchen of his Los Angeles home.

Complacent aficionados of rare wines had erroneously assumed that there could never be another fine wine fraud perpetuated at the level that Hardy Rodenstock had achieved. But Kurniawan proved them wrong.

Like Rodenstock before him, he had initially

impressed fine wine experts and journalists with his sophisticated palate and scholarly knowledge.

Dr. Conti, as he was nicknamed in fine wine circles, due to his predilection for the wines from Domaine-de-La Romanee-Conti (DRC), took the collector market by storm.

He hosted lavish tastings of fabled wines, and with his brash big-hitter bidding style at auctions, he quickly made a name for himself amongst preeminent connoisseurs.

Rudy was an elite Hermes customer, and a veritable walking billboard for the brand.

His refined taste in exotic cars led to his being selected as one of the participants in a road rally through the California wine country organized by the prestigious Robb Report lifestyle magazine. He amassed a world class art collection.

Seemingly, Rudy epitomized the image of a jet set connoisseur, who was the eccentric heir of an affluent Indonesian family, and he successfully hoodwinked sophisticated wine collectors and wine auction houses who vied for his business.

In 2016, there was yet another major controversy in Burgundy.

The négociant firm, *Maison Béjot Vins-et-Terroirs*, which owned the well-known labels—*Chartron et Trébuchet*, Pierre André, Reine Pédauque, Moillard, and *Domaine-du-Chapitre* in Beaujolais; was raided due to suspicions of fraud by customs officers, led by Claude Leveque.

All told, since the 1970s, the cumulative amount of adulterated and fake wine foisted on a gullible worldwide marketplace was staggering.

The well-publicized stories about the high-profile fraudsters- Hardy Rodenstock and Rudy Kurniawan, who created and dealt in concocted rarities, persisted in the public conscious.

But the much larger problem of fraud in the wine trade, which was perpetuated in far greater volumes by wineries and brokers, always seemed to fade from collected memory far too quickly, even though the commercial abuses dwarfed the more sensationalized individual criminal acts.

But Claude Leveque was now fully aware of the extent of the problem, and he was energized to root out all the offenders!

CHAPTER ELEVEN

"Wine makes every meal an occasion, every table
more elegant, every day more civilized."
Andre Simon

Pierre Ducler and Maurice Blanchard had grown
up together in the Burgundian town of Aloxe-
Corton.

They were like brothers and shared a bond of
friendship as strong as any blood tie.

Immersed in the local wine culture from an early
age, they both shared a passion for the wines of
Burgundy and pursued formal training through the
time-honored apprentice systems prevalent in France,
and throughout Europe.

While Pierre's focus as a *sommelier* was on
education and service, Maurice was enamored with
the subtle and elaborate processes involved in the art

of fine winemaking, and he had also studied at the prestigious *Université-de-Bourgogne* in Dijon.

Though talented and outgoing with an engaging personality, Pierre grew up in the shadow of his autocratic father who had been a successful exporter representing boutique *domaines*.

Pierre had learned to cope with the insecurities created from constant reminders of his allegedly unfulfilled promise, and from a history of his relatives disappointing him.

When his father died unexpectedly, Pierre's family squabbled over the estate, and they decided to sell the business rather than perpetuate it.

By the time the burdensome taxes were paid, and the remaining proceeds divided up, little remained.

After months of soul searching, Pierre realized that trying to live up to his father's legacy was not his burden to bear.

Instead, he decided to follow his own path and train as a *sommelier*.

Pierre, in the role of *de facto* older sibling, provided Maurice with his primary source of advice and feedback about his winemaking, and Maurice habitually shared ideas and wine samples with Pierre to elicit his opinions.

I was devastated to learn of Maurice's passing.

I immediately called Pierre to express my sympathies, and to arrange to fly over for the funeral.

When I arrived at the airport in Dijon, which was a former air force base, I rented a car and drove to meet Pierre.

We had agreed to rendezvous late that afternoon at

one of the *Chateau de La Rochepot* vineyards.

As I arrived at the vineyard, the adjoining Chateau loomed against a darkening sky.

On the ramparts above, I chanced to see Hans Gauner looking down at us, a self-styled lord observing his *domaine.*

I waved to him. With a perfunctory wave back, and an inscrutable expression on his face, he departed.

I greeted Pierre, and after we exchanged initial requisite pleasantries and heartfelt regrets for the loss of Maurice, he suggested that we walk together.

As we ambled through the vineyard, I could see that Pierre was understandably deeply troubled about the circumstances of Maurice's death.

He was in a pensive mood, and seemed hard-pressed about how best to express what was weighing on him.

He stopped to pry a plump snail off one of the vines.

Using a small knife, he extricated it from its shell and ate it with an unappetizing slurping sound.

Once finished, with an almost imperceptible nod he proceeded to share his thoughts with me.

According to Pierre, Maurice had worked at the *Chateau de La Rochepot* as the winemaker for a year prior to Gauner's acquisition of the property.

At Gauner's insistence, Maurice had stayed on and continued his work.

For a time, everything had seemed to go smoothly.

Gauner provided capital to improve the vineyards, but the cellars and winemaking equipment remained traditional and artisanal, befitting the small production and status of the wines.

When Maurice returned to the *chateau* to prepare for the harvest after a month's vacation, he had noticed that some unexpected changes had transpired at the property.

On the day prior to his death, he had confided to Pierre, without going into specifics, that some things he had discovered had disturbed him.

Pierre never learned any further details, and while he had no specific reason to suspect foul play, and the police had quickly dismissed his concerns, the coincident timing of Maurice's passing troubled him.

Even though the formal police review had been closed, we agreed to do some investigating of our own...

CHAPTER TWELVE

"I drink to make other people more interesting."
Ernest Hemingway

When I checked into the hotel, there was a missive waiting for me from Herr Gauner requesting that I join him for dinner that evening at the *chateau*.

After his restrained greeting from afar that afternoon, I was surprised at the invitation, but I called and confirmed that I would attend.

I arrived at the chateau and spoke with *Le Nez* through the intercom at the entrance gate.

He was waiting for me at the front door and beckoned me into the dining room.

The long, imposing table was decorated with silver candelabras and set for two.

Four oversized crystal wine glasses, glimmering invitingly in the candlelight, awaited us at each place setting.

Le Nez explained that Herr Gauner would join me momentarily, and asked me to be seated.

A man I had not seen before appeared and poured me a glass of white wine, and invited me to taste it.

I noticed that he had an unusual accent. I couldn't place the origin, but I thought that it sounded Slavic.

As I awaited Gauner, I sampled the white wine.

The bouquet reminded me of the fresh mineral smell of spring water rushing over river rocks. I guessed it to be a fine example of Chablis.

Gauner entered the room elegantly attired for dinner in a well-cut conservative chalk-striped English suit, looking every inch the successful international entrepreneur.

He greeted me effusively like a long-lost friend and asked how I liked the wine.

When I suggested that I thought it to be an excellent Chablis, he nodded sagely, but declined to reveal the name.

I assumed that he had organized a secret theme for the wines he was serving, and I looked forward to trying to decipher the challenge.

Over small talk, we enjoyed perfectly chilled raw Belan oysters with what was obviously an excellent Champagne.

This wine resonated in my mind as a *Blanc-de-Blancs* with creamy overtones that perfectly suited the shellfish.

When Gauner raised his glass for a toast to our reacquaintance, the persistent stream of fine bubbles glowed in the moonlight, resembling a magical fireworks display.

The next wine, which was served with a delicious *Poulet-de-Bresse*, brought back evocative memories of the smells of the vineyard air and soil in Chambolle-Musigny, as well as of the personalities of the people I had previously met there.

Wine appreciation can be a conduit to deep thoughts and animated conversation.

As we dined, Gauner casually remarked that several years ago, a Princeton economist had come up with an algorithm based on yearly grape crop weather data that nearly exactly mimicked Robert Parker's vintage scores.

We both chuckled at this, and I realized that there is a danger in getting to know your adversary too well, and forming feelings of empathy and shared understanding.

Our next course was *Ris-de-Veau*. The sweetbreads perfectly complemented the accompanying wine which reminded me of a fine old Chambertin.

I mused that revisiting a memorable wine that one has not sampled for some time is like rekindling an old friendship.

When Gauner observed that the wine still smelled tannic, I refrained from comment, but noted to myself that I had now evened the score with Herr Gauner for his previous disdain about how I had eaten my fish at the dinner where we had first met, because you cannot smell tannin!

As I continued my vinous evaluation, Gauner

became more outspoken.

I listened to him ever more dramatically espousing his opinions.

His inflated and narcissistic ego reminded me of Napoleon Bonaparte, who I remembered had appreciated Chambertin.

Gauner excessively swirled and agitated the wine in his glass into an angry red foam, as he complained about journalists who he felt were self-proclaimed arbiters of taste that passed off their arbitrary assessments and judgments as incontestable facts.

By this point, I was keen to learn if my wine guesses had been accurate, but it was evidently Gauner's plan to string me along for a bit longer.

He suggested that we adjourn to the wine cellar for some *Marc-de-Bourgogne* so that he could show me his wine collection.

Given my impression that Gauner was fastidious in his habits, I expected to encounter wine storage organized with Teutonic precision.

I was therefore taken aback as we descended the steep stairs to encounter a damp tomb-like chill in a cavernous dank chamber where a layer of slimy mold grew on some areas of the walls.

Ancient well-used barrels showed signs of rot.

Along one wall were four huge old decayed oak fermentation casks.

Hundreds of bottles with thick layers of dust occupied rows of bins, and appeared to have not been disturbed for many years.

Mind you, I like a cellar with a bit of character.

I am not enamored by overly antiseptic

winemaking facilities that are soulless shrines to technology.

I am all for the subtle earthy, vinous smells that thrive in cellars with suitably cool and humid conditions.

But this cellar exhibited signs of deferred maintenance and neglect.

Gauner moved aside a few dilapidated wooden crates and indicated I should follow him to a previously obscured non-descript doorway at the far end of the room.

When he opened the door, bright white light filled the opening, and I heard a faint humming sound from within.

Looking back at me as he passed through, he invited me to come see his most secret vinous treasures...

CHAPTER THIRTEEN

"He who knows how to taste does not drink wine but
savours secrets."
Salvador Dali

As we entered the impressive inner sanctum,
Gauner introduced me with a flourish of his
arms to his laboratory.

Everywhere I looked gleaming equipment was
being overseen by white lab-coated attendants.

At first, I thought this must be Gauner's perfume
laboratory.

But as I took in further details, I saw a line of large
rolling carts filled with wine bottles.

Perhaps this was just a new wine production facility
that I had previously been unaware of, but with slight
puzzlement, I realized that the evident scale of

production far exceeded the limited amount of wine that *Chateau de La Rochepot* produced and bottled.

Gauner interrupted my reverie to belatedly ask me to identify the dinner wines.

My response was: a ten-year old Chablis, likely a Grand Cru; a vintage *Blanc-de-Blancs* Champagne, possibly from Cramant, and also approximately ten years old; a Grand Cru red Burgundy from the *Cotes-de-Nuits*, most likely a Musigny from 1988 or 1990.

And the last wine must be another superlative bottle of the exquisite 1964 Chambertin that Gauner had previously shared with me on the night we had first met.

Gauner nodded his approval. "Very good," he exclaimed.

"As I previously observed, you have an excellent palate!

"That is exactly what each of these wines was supposed to taste like.

"But all of them were created yesterday here in my laboratory!"

Taken aback, I listened with growing apprehension as Gauner explained that he had determined the ultimate methods to artificially recreate wines, so perfectly rendered that they were impossible to tell from the originals.

He went to a table and poured water from a pitcher into two wine glasses, and offered one to me.

I observed that as he continued to speak, he absentmindedly swirled his water glass, as if it held wine.

Then, as he continued, he covered the bowl portion

of the glass with his hands to raise the temperature of the contents.

"I would like you to represent us in America and be our importer. I can make you a very rich man!

"What I suggest is really no different than what many people in your business already do, and have done for many years—turn a blind eye to wines that are not really what they purport to be, when they represent opportunities to reap significant profits, with consumers none the wiser.

"Let me show you around the facility and introduce you to my team."

CHAPTER FOURTEEN

"Wine is sunlight, held together by water."
Galileo Galilei

B ottle variation in older wines makes conclusive identification of fakes exceedingly difficult.
    As wines evolve, even bottles that have been stored identically, and removed from the same case, can taste remarkably different.

Differences in provenance result in even more variability.

Hardy Rodenstock and Rudy Kurniawan had proved that even "experts" could be fooled.

Disturbingly, while the branding and packaging of a wine is subject to copyright, the contents of a bottle, and what it tastes like, is not.

There is still no foolproof analytical technique for verifying precise vintage and geographical provenance.

Once a wine is consumed, the evidence is gone forever.

But this was no amateurish vinous fraud perpetuated from an improvised kitchen workshop.

Unlike the charlatans who blended less expensive vintages from a famed property to approximate the bouquet and flavors of a much more heralded and pricey year, or skillfully mixed other wines with similar characteristics to achieve a plausible facsimile, this level of deceit was far more sophisticated.

State of the art forgery, creating exacting duplicates of valuable wines on an unprecedented scale using advanced scientific nanotechnology techniques to identify the molecular base components, and flawlessly replicate them.

So well-conceived and executed that it was virtually impossible to detect.

In retrospect, the large-scale commercial manipulation of wine for profit perhaps most noticeably began in perfectly legal fashion with the use of soaking oak chips in wine.

An expedient subterfuge to cost-effectively duplicate the flavors of expensive oak barrel aging.

With Hans' experience as a fine wine collector, and his vast knowledge in the perfume business, he already had the insights and sophisticated equipment to begin engineering synthetic wine.

His motivation was not merely greed. Just like Rodenstock and Kurniawan, he thrived on the opportunity to secretly prove his superior intellect, by duping pompous critics and wealthy, egotistical collectors.

Starting with his protégé *Le Nez's* expertise in creating complex fragrances, Gauner carefully assembled a team of hand-picked experts to implement a level of technically sophisticated vinous fraud that would completely fool any analysis.

George Carter was trained as a chemist. He was a rotund man with swept back blond hair and a perpetual artificial tan.

He was a flavorist by trade, and had previously worked for Givaudan and Cargill, in businesses very similar to the perfume industry, where he had created flavors for a wide variety of foods, beverages, confections, pharmaceuticals, and oral care products including vitamins, toothpaste, lip balm, mouth wash, chewable medications and liquid prescriptions.

He had also worked at a small laboratory in California for a startup company that had pioneered techniques to chemically synthesize wine.

Flavor engineering is an arcane and secretive process.

Chemists like Carter work to create flavorings that consumers will find delicious, appealing and addicting.

Carter was experienced in using mathematical formulas to blend aromatic chemicals, essential oils, botanical extracts and essences, measured in minute quantities of parts per million, to create specific tastes using precise mixtures of synthetic and natural chemicals.

While taste is defined as a chemical sense perceived by receptor cells and interpreted by the brain, flavor is a more elusive concept that combines gustatory, olfactory, tactile, thermal, and even pain sensitivity, with texture and consistency.

There are at least 2,000 flavor compounds and 500 natural flavors available commercially, each composed of chemicals, or chemical blends.

In conjunction with our sense of smell, 100,000 taste buds discern sensations of sweetness, bitterness, sourness and saltiness.

Traditionally, most wine is made by fermenting grapes.

Yeast turns sugars in the grape must into ethanol.

A bottle of wine usually contains around 1,000 different compounds.

Some flavor compounds, like fatty acids and esters, are challenging to dissolve straight into a synthetic batch, since they are normally produced when microbes process the fermentation, gradually releasing chemicals in forms that are able to mix with the other compounds that are present.

To establish the chemical combinations for the flavor of a specific wine, Carter used gas and liquid chromatography, mass spectrometry, and other tools common in the world of perfumes and food science, to analyze, isolate and identify the chemical makeup of a wine.

He would burn a wine sample in a gas chromatograph.

This would release a vapor that he would filter into a spectrometer.

The molecules would pass through the spectrometer in order of weight and size, allowing him to identify their concentrations.

Then he would ignore the molecules that didn't make any contribution to taste, and record the core chemical building blocks of that wine's flavor, so that he could replicate them with natural or synthetic chemicals.

Using this list of molecular ingredients and percentages, he could then build a complete synthetic version, mixing these molecules and tinkering with minute adjustments to the proportions.

Ethanol, water, sugars, acids, glycerin, wood and fruit tannins, esters and other organic wine-flavor compound chemicals, and their concentrations in purified forms, were carefully combined with a proprietary mix of amino acids.

He used ethyl isobutyrate and ethyl hexanoate to contribute fruity, pineapple-like aromas. Sotolon provided a caramel taste.

Methoxypyrazine lent a distinctive green bell pepper note.

Rotundone exuded the classic black peppery aromas typically found in Syrah.

Isoamylacetate mimicked the banana and apple aromas which are traditionally the result of skin contact.

Diacetyl evoked buttery flavors and aromas. He used methoxyfuraneol to simulate the scent of strawberries.

Carter even mastered the recreation of the unique barnyard smells and flavors evocative of brettanomyces, and the tainted smell of corked wine from trichloroanisole.

He used varying levels of sulphur dioxide to exactly adjust and mimic the level of detectable sulfites for each wine.

To replicate ancient wines, Carter had installed a hermetically sealed chamber which conformed to the Federal Institute for Materials Research and Testing standards.

He prepared these wines so that they would successfully pass scientific carbon dating testing with tritium, carbon-14 and cesium-137.

Pristine, unused original labels for many wines were often surprisingly easy to acquire.

Importers and wholesalers had filing cabinets filled with old labels for use in captain's book restaurant wine lists which could be covertly purchased from employees seeking to augment their income.

Wineries also routinely disposed of labels with superseded designs which they no longer needed.

Gauner had methodically stock-piled hundreds of boxes, with thousands of original labels for prestigious wines, just waiting to be used.

He purchased state of the art offset and intaglio printing presses for his team to use when they needed to create labels in-house so that they perfectly matched the originals.

Gauner enlisted the talents of a short, stocky, pale-faced currency and document forger from the Ukraine named Uri Yanuk, who was well-versed in the nuances of inks, engraving, holograms, security threads, see-through registers, iridescent stripes, shifting colors and watermarks.

Yanuk was a disciple of famed British master forger Charles Black.

After Black's incarceration, Yanuk had secretly worked with notorious Canadian counterfeiter Frank Bourassa, who had successfully created over 200 million dollars in fake US currency that was identical to real banknotes.

Using the same German paper mill that Bourassa had used, Yanuk secured quantities of paper stocks made to his specifications with various blends of cotton, cellulose and linen which exactly matched the different papers used by top wineries, and that would stand up to any black light test or modern security feature.

Then, working with Carter, he researched and tested hundreds of different glues to be sure the versions they used for each type of wine label precisely matched the originals.

Using corks obtained from several sources in Portugal, cut to exact lengths as required, he branded them as needed with exact copies of winery logos and vintages from an extensive archive of designs.

Yanuk was tantalized by the opportunity to become uber rich through wine fraud.

Compared to the challenges and risks of successfully forging intricately detailed currency papers and images, accurately replicating wine labels for him was child's play.

The profit from selling bottles of wine worth thousands of dollars was much more interesting than making a third of the face value of forged $20 and

$100 bills on the black market.

After the tour of the lab, Gauner and I returned to the old cellar.

As we walked by the large fermenting casks, he casually pointed to the cask at the far end and remarked that it was the one where Maurice had died.

He looked at me with cold blue eyes, empty of any visible emotion.

Carefully evaluating me, he said, "It was tragic to lose such a talented young winemaker.

"I regret that he declined to embrace our plans for expansion.

"I hope you take my meaning."

To which I replied, "Yes I understand what you are implying. "We have no misunderstanding."

"Good," said Gauner. "It's very important that you clearly understand your choices."

CHAPTER FIFTEEN

"This is one of the disadvantages of wine, it makes a
man mistake words for thoughts."
Samuel Johnson

As was the case at many French vineyards, at the
Chateau de La Rochepot seasonal migrant
workers came every year to pick the grapes.

Though industrious, some of them could be hot-
blooded, unpredictable, and larcenous.

Reports of thievery, and of heated arguments and
knife fights at their camps in the evenings, were not
unusual.

I learned to my detriment that Gauner employed
one of them for other tasks as well.

Vano was a lean, dark-skinned man with a flashing
smile and dark impenetrable brown eyes. A long scar

decorated one of his cheekbones.

After my encounter with Gauner, I arranged to meet Pierre the next morning to apprise him about what I had learned.

Out of a lack of prudence, and caught up in our emotions, we made a very foolish decision.

Pierre informed me that he had found out that Gauner would be making a rare appearance at a local *fete* that evening celebrating the success of the recent harvest.

Pierre had a key for an exterior door to the winery at Rochepot, that he had found in Maurice's small home, called a *chaumière*.

We agreed to go to the *chateau* as soon as Gauner departed for the event, to try to find evidence that we could use to convince the police to raid the laboratory.

As we watched from afar, we saw Gauner and his entourage depart for the celebration.

We hadn't expected anyone to be inside the winery at this late hour. And no one was awaiting us there.

But unbeknownst to me, Vano had been following me all day...

When we entered the upper entryway to the cellar and began to look around, we were alarmed to hear the sound of the lock to the entrance door being bolted behind us.

We turned and saw Vano confidently smiling at us as he pulled an evil-looking knife from his pocket, and then he proceeded to methodically stalk toward us.

As Vano approached Pierre with ill-intent, things would no doubt have gone very badly for us, were it not for blind luck.

As Vano closed the distance, Pierre had his back to the moldy wall, sliding to the side in a vain effort to try and avoid his fate.

In desperation, I dove at Vano, and as he turned cat-like and struck out at me, finding his mark in my shoulder, we ended up in a heap in a corner against a horse-drawn plow.

Vano was impaled and eviscerated by the sharp blade of the plow.

I rolled away from him as he stared at his exposed entrails in disbelief...

CHAPTER SIXTEEN

"A man will be eloquent if you give him good wine."
Ralph Waldo Emerson

As I watched Vano's eyes glaze over, Pierre came to me and tried to staunch the flow of blood from my shoulder.

While I held Pierre's handkerchief against the wound, he called the local *gendarmerie*, and the hospital.

By the time the *gendarmes* and paramedics arrived, I was delirious and incoherent.

Dimly I was aware that the orderlies picked me up and put me on a stretcher.

As they carried me to the ambulance, I overheard one of the policemen pronounce Vano dead.

Pierre walked to the ambulance with me, but was

prevented from going with us to the clinic.

As the ambulance was departing, with a look of concern Pierre told me that he would come to the hospital as soon as the police had finished taking his statement and released him.

CHAPTER SEVENTEEN

"In Vino Veritas."
Pliny the Elder

The next morning, as I lay in my hospital bed recovering, the police came to interview me, accompanied by a shabby-looking plain clothes inspector named Claude Leveque, who reeked of nicotine.

Leveque proceeded to question me at great length, making copious notes in an official-looking folder.

They then allowed Pierre to visit me, and he related what had transpired after the ambulance had taken me away.

The police had found the entrance to the laboratory, and when an astonished Gauner had returned to the *chateau* later that night, the officers, with Inspector Leveque who had joined them, were waiting to arrest him and his cohorts.

To our consternation, under penalty of imprisonment, both Pierre and I were admonished by the police and Leveque not to discuss what we knew about the situation with anyone.

Just before I was released from the hospital, Leveque returned with a dour-looking civil servant, who, to our dismay, informed Pierre and me that our bags had been packed, and we were being taken to the airport to be flown to an undisclosed location.

Leveque had us sign papers attesting that we would never reveal any details about what we had seen or experienced.

Then, without any further explanation, he gave me a plain blank envelope filled with high denomination Euros for "traveling money", and told us that someone would be in touch to check on us when we arrived at our destination.

As the two officials were departing, Leveque hesitated for a moment at the doorway.

He looked back at us with a reproachful look, an unspoken reminder of his warning not to divulge any information, a visual reminder of the severe consequences if we did so...

EPILOGUE

"Wine gave a sort of gallantry to their own failure."
F. Scott Fitzgerald

Wine production is France's most valuable agronomical product, representing 7.6 billion Euros annually. It amounts to 15% of the nation's overall agricultural revenue, and employs over 500,000 people, not including additional seasonal migrant labor.

Twenty-four million tourists visit the French wine regions each year.

Multinational companies that sell luxury goods, such as premium wine and perfume brands, many of which are French based, are always anxious to avoid any negative publicity.

And it would at the least be unseemly to have a significant historic property which had been owned by a former French president's family tied to such a disgrace.

The French government decided to quietly cover up the Gauner scandal, in order to save face, and to prevent any embarrassing attention for them or these companies.

They wanted to circumvent consumer backlash, and the possibility of another major collapse of the French fine wine market, on an even greater scale than what had previously occurred in Bordeaux due to the Cruse scandal, and from the multiple similarly disruptive exposés in Burgundy.

According to the documents released from the investigation, the ownership of the *Chateau de La Rochepot* was in the name of a Luxembourg-based corporation.

The detectives assigned to the case later claimed to have established that the ultimate owner was a Ukrainian fugitive named Dmytro Malinovsky who they had arrested at the chateau.

Malinovsky was wanted by the authorities in his homeland in connection with outstanding warrants for a major fraud and forgery case involving Defense Ministry property.

When it subsequently came to light that a death certificate had previously been filed for Malinovsky several years before, the prosecutor's office responded that this certificate had been forged by Malinovsky as a ruse to escape justice.

Today, the *Chateau de La Rochepot* is owned by

the French Ministry of Culture.

"My only regret in life is that I did not drink more wine."
Ernest Hemingway

Please enjoy the prologue of
Derailed Gears

PROLOGUE

(In cycling, a prologue is a short preliminary time trial held
before a race to establish a leader)

L ate one night, Ernesto Sante was laboring in his
small makeshift workshop, to finish building a
custom lightweight steel racing bicycle frame,
for famed local racer—Gino Fausto, the favorite
to win the upcoming prestigious *Giro d'Italia*
competition.

Sante, who had been nicknamed The Tailor by the
European racing community, was a legendary builder.

He possessed extraordinary skill at creating short
wheelbase racing frames, with stiff, catlike handling,
that, due to the meticulous bespoke measurements for
the rider's physique, were surprisingly comfortable to
ride over long distances.

An important attribute for grueling races such as
the *Giro*.

He was a true craftsman, and his frames not only
consistently performed well, but were also beautiful to
behold.

Unlike the famed French *constructeurs*, who, in the 1950s, were for the most part focused on building filet-brazed lugless touring bicycles, with elaborate braze-ons to attach proprietary components- for racing bikes, Italian frames had become the preferred choice amongst many top competitors, and Sante was recognized as one of the elite artisans.

Sante favored bright colors for his frames, devoid of pinstriping and contrasting panels, to highlight his signature Florentine *fleur-de-lis* cutouts, which he engraved by hand in the minimalist hand-shaped, and painstakingly filed and finished lugs, with elegant shorelines.

His detailing, was much subtler than the complex embellishments favored by many British frame makers at that time, which resembled the elaborate curvilinear designs of fine sterling silver culinary utensils, and intricately engraved bespoke shotgun sideplates.

Sante's brazing technique, included the use of both bronze rod for the thicker metal of bottom brackets and dropouts, and nickel silver for the much thinner-walled lug joinery.

Most Italian builders used domestically made Columbus tubing, exclusively for their projects, but Sante always combined a proprietary mix of both Columbus, and British Reynolds tubing for each build, specifically chosen for each rider's physique, and the intended use for the frame.

He eschewed using a frame jig, which he felt placed unwanted stress on the tubing, and could cause subsequent warping and hairline cracks.

He preferred to build completely by eye, constantly checking trueness against the hand drawn plans he custom designed for each client.

When it was time to proceed with the brazing, he turned on his oxyacetylene tanks, and lighting the torch, he adjusted the flow of the gasses.

He further fine-tuned the combination of oxygen, and acetylene to create optimum inner and outer envelopes of flame.

As he began to heat the area where the chainstays were inserted into the bottom bracket, he was disturbed to hear an unusual hissing sound emanating from the area where the gas tanks were standing.

In all his years of brazing, he had never discerned such a sound before...

Irritated, because the bottom bracket had now reached the perfect shade of cherry red to begin filling in the voids with the bronze rod, he pulled back from his work to look at the tanks and hoses, to determine what was causing the discordant sound.

As he turned with torch in hand, he was aghast, to hear, and see, the roar of an ignited conflagration, and feel a concussive explosion.

These were the final impressions in the fading conscious of The Tailor...

ABOUT THE AUTHOR

E. Robert Brooks has over 35 years of experience in the fine wine trade purchasing, selling, and managing significant inventories of investment grade fine wine.

He began his career in France working for the négociant firm Maison Ginestet at Chateau Margaux for the 1976 harvest. Edward continued from there to work in the Ginestet cellars in Bordeaux and was involved in the selection of wines for the Air France Concorde flights. He then went on to Germany for a similar apprenticeship with H. Sichel Sohne in Mainz.

Additionally, Brooks has worked in the wholesale distribution side of the business having held the title of Fine Wine Director at Chicago based Judge and Dolph, Ltd. He also spent over seven years working with noted importers- Remy Amerique as their Fine Wine Specialist in Chicago, and as the Central Regional Manager for Frederick Wildman and Sons.

He has managed several major fine wine auction houses. He was Christie's Department Head of Wine for the Americas, and Director of Fine Wine Auctions for Phillips. He founded Edward Roberts International, and served as Managing Director and

Managing Auctioneer for ten years.

Upon selling the company to Acker, Merrall and Condit; for several years he continued on as Midwest Managing Director and Managing Auctioneer.

These days, Brooks runs a fine wine investment fund named- Grande Marque Trading LLC, and oversees the preeminent website for fine wine data- wineauctionprices.com

Printed in Poland
by Amazon Fulfillment
Poland Sp. z o.o., Wrocław
16 December 2022

9aa241bd-4408-4b21-9985-da000e8fa5d5R01